Written By
Neil Gaiman & Adam Rex

Illustrated By

Chu's First Day at School

BLOOMSBURY

LONDON NEW DELHI NEW YORK SYDNEY

For Ronan.
–N.G.

For Jack.
–A.R.

Bloomsbury Publishing, London, New Delhi, New York and Sydney
First published in Great Britain in 2014 by Bloomsbury Publishing Plc
50 Bedford Square, London, WC1B 3DP

First published in the US in 2014 by HarperCollins Children's Books, a division of
HarperCollins Publishers, 10 East 53rd Street, New York, NY 10022

Text copyright © Neil Gaiman 2014
Illustrations copyright © Adam Rex 2014
The moral right of the author and illustrator has been asserted

A CIP catalogue record of this book is available from the British Library

ISBN 978 1 4088 4703 9

Printed in China by Leo Paper Products, Heshan, Guangdong
13 5 7 9 10 8 6 4 2

All papers used by Bloomsbury Publishing are natural, recyclable products made from
wood grown in well-managed forests. The manufacturing processes conform to
the environmental regulations of the country of origin

www.bloomsbury.com

BLOOMSBURY is a registered trademark of Bloomsbury Publishing Plc

There was a thing
that Chu could do.

Chu was worried. He had never been to school before.
"What will happen?" Chu asked his father. "Will they be nice?"
"They will be nice."

"Will they like me?" Chu asked his mother.
"Of course they will like you," she told him.

Chu hoped they were right.

After breakfast his parents took him to the school.
There were other boys and girls there.

The teacher
had a
friendly face.

She showed them where the toys were, and where they would sit.

"Now," she said, "I want each of you to tell the class your name, and I will write it down on the blackboard. You must say one thing that you love to do."

"My name is Jengo.
I like to get things down
from high places.
What do YOU do?"

Chu didn't say anything.

"My name is Pablo. I love to climb up things.
I can climb trees, if they are not too big.
What do YOU do?"

Chu didn't say anything.

"My name is Robin.
I can sing and I can fly.
I love to sing.
What do YOU do?"

Chu didn't say anything.

"My name is Tiny.
I like to go into my room and close the
door and not come out until I want to.
What do YOU do?"

One by one they went around the whole class.
They all had something special that they did.
They loved to dance, or to be funny,
or to run very fast, or to read books,
or to hang upside down.

The teacher wrote each name on the blackboard in chalk.
She needed more space to write.
She rubbed out things that had been on
the blackboard before.

There was a lot of
chalk dust in the air.

Now only one person was left.
"Hello, little panda," said the teacher. "Tell us about you."

"My name is Chu."

AAH-

AAAAH-

AAAAAH-

AAaachoOOO

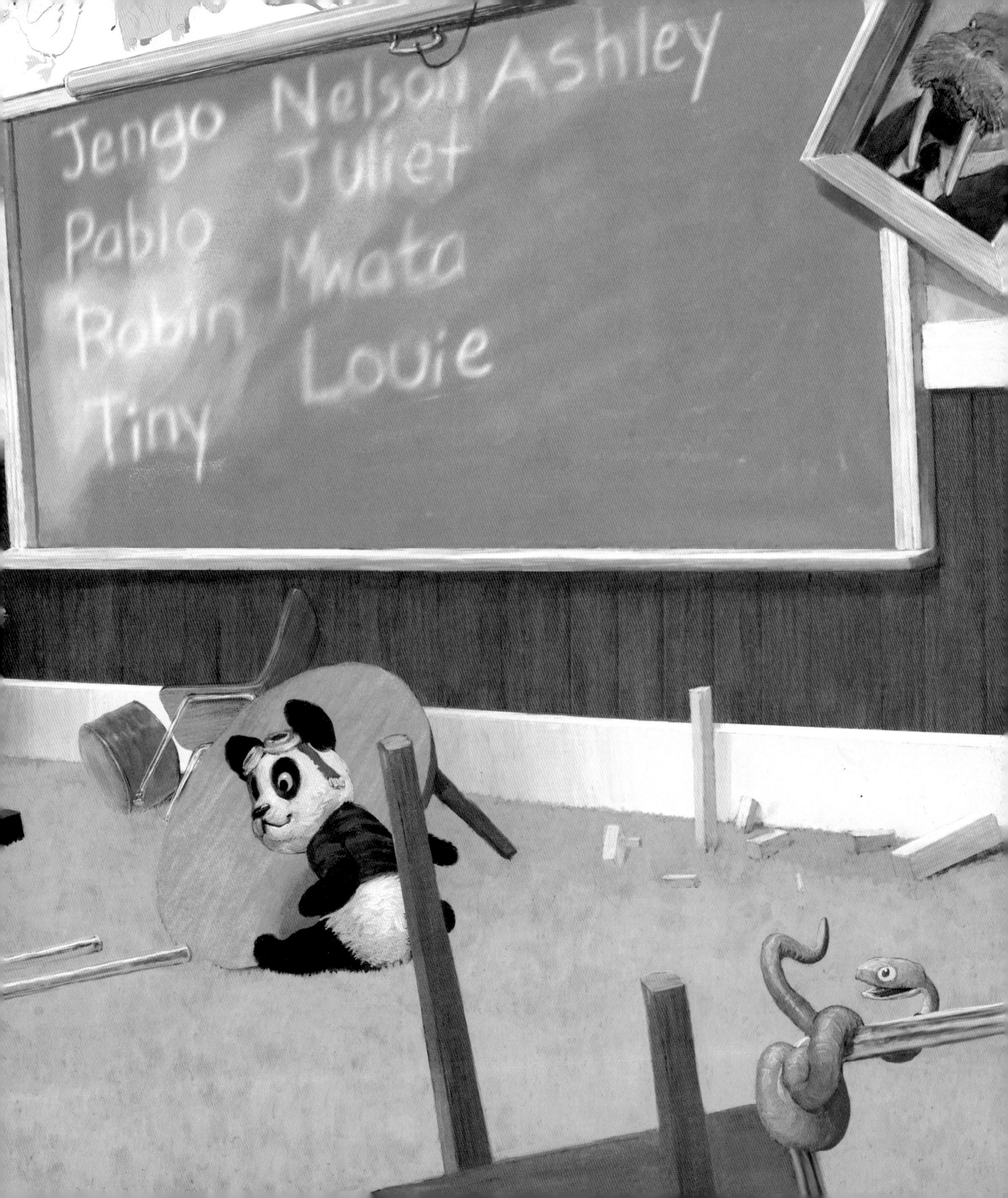
Jengo
Nelson
Ashley
Juliet
Pablo
Mwata
Robin
Louie
Tiny

"*That's* what I do."

"How was school?" asked his father.
"It was pretty good," said Chu.

"Did they like you?"
asked his mother.

"They liked me," said Chu.
"They were nice.
I'm not worried anymore."

Goodnight.